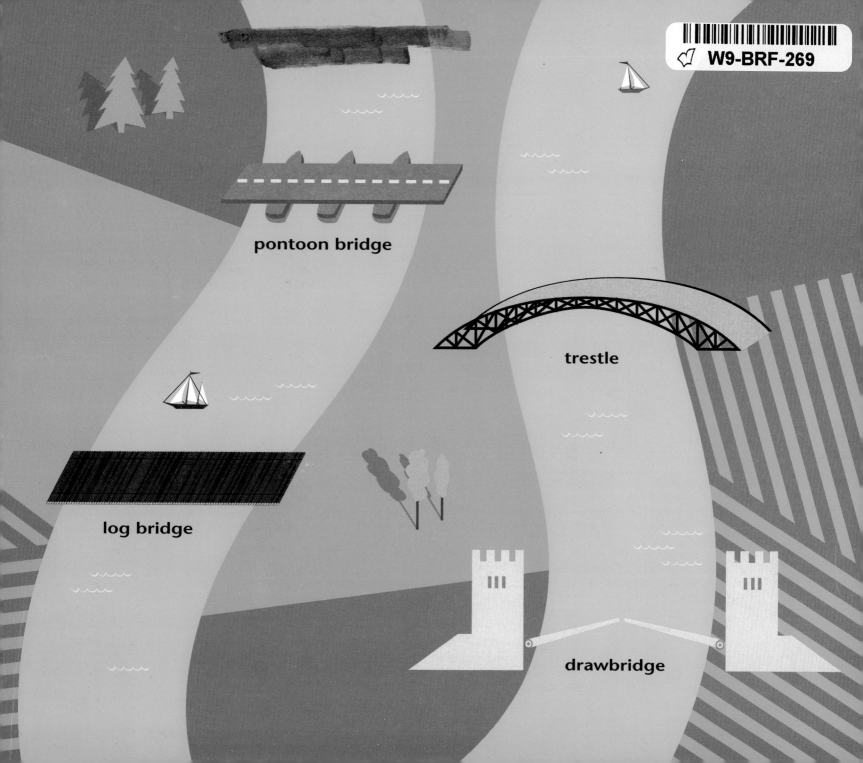

pontoon bridge

trestle

log bridge

drawbridge

CROSS A BRIDGE

by Ryan Ann Hunter

illustrated by Edward Miller

Holiday House / New York

In memory of my parents, and to Uncle Jack —E. G. M.

Thanks, Walter, for crossing bridges with me —P. D. G.

To my nephew Steven Cox —E. M.

Text copyright © 1998 by Pamela D. Greenwood and Elizabeth G. Macalaster
Illustrations copyright © 1998 by Edward Miller III
All rights reserved
Printed in the United States of America
First Edition

Library of Congress Cataloging-in-Publication Data
Hunter, Ryan Ann.
    Cross a bridge / by Ryan Ann Hunter; illustrated by Edward Miller III
— 1st ed.
            p.   cm.
    Summary: Describes different kinds of bridges: how they are built and
how they are used.
    ISBN 0-8234-1340-3
    1. Bridges—Juvenile literature. [1. Bridges.] I. Miller, Ed, 1964– ill.
TG148.H86   1998
624' .2—dc21   97-1265   CIP   AC

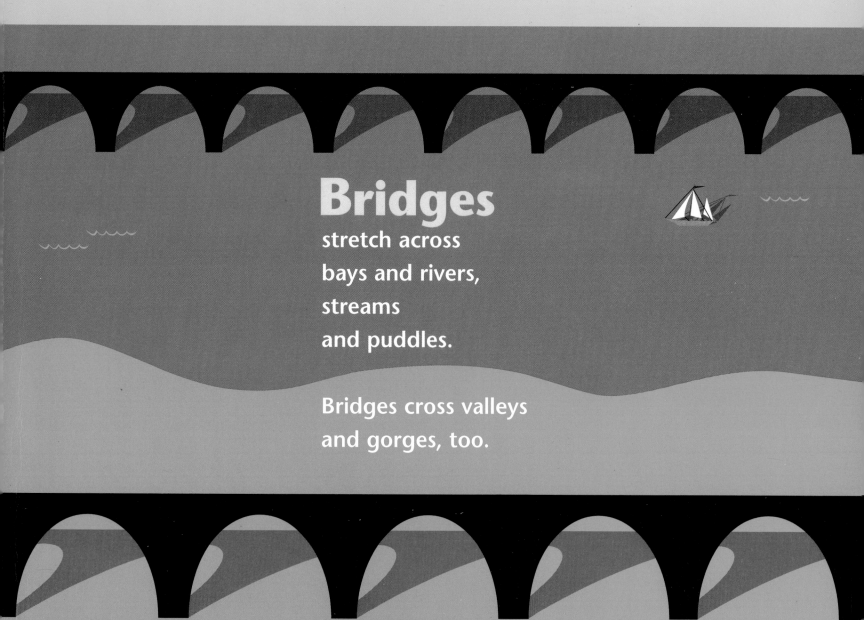

Bridges
**stretch across
bays and rivers,
streams
and puddles.**

Bridges cross valleys
and gorges, too.

Bridges used to be made
from just about anything:

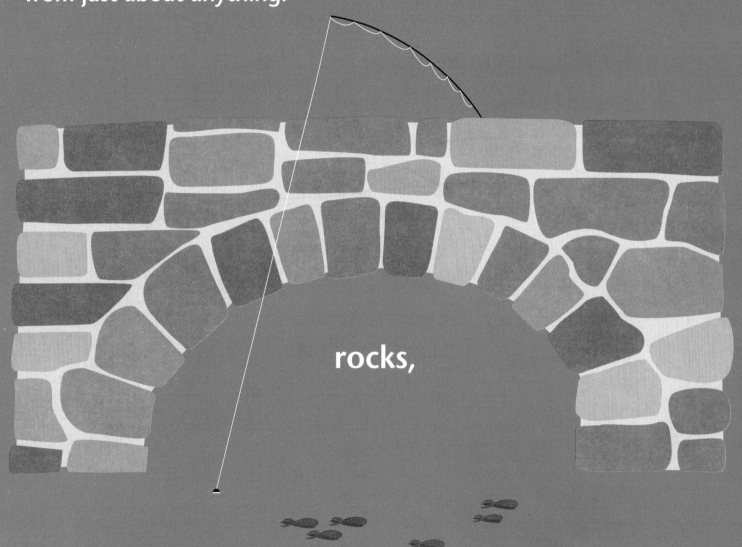

rocks,

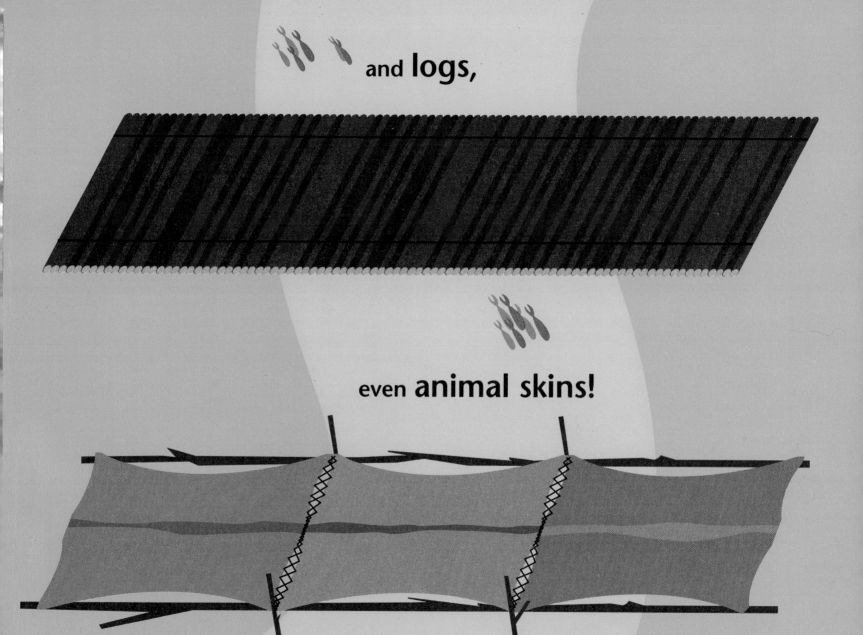

and **logs,**

even **animal skins!**

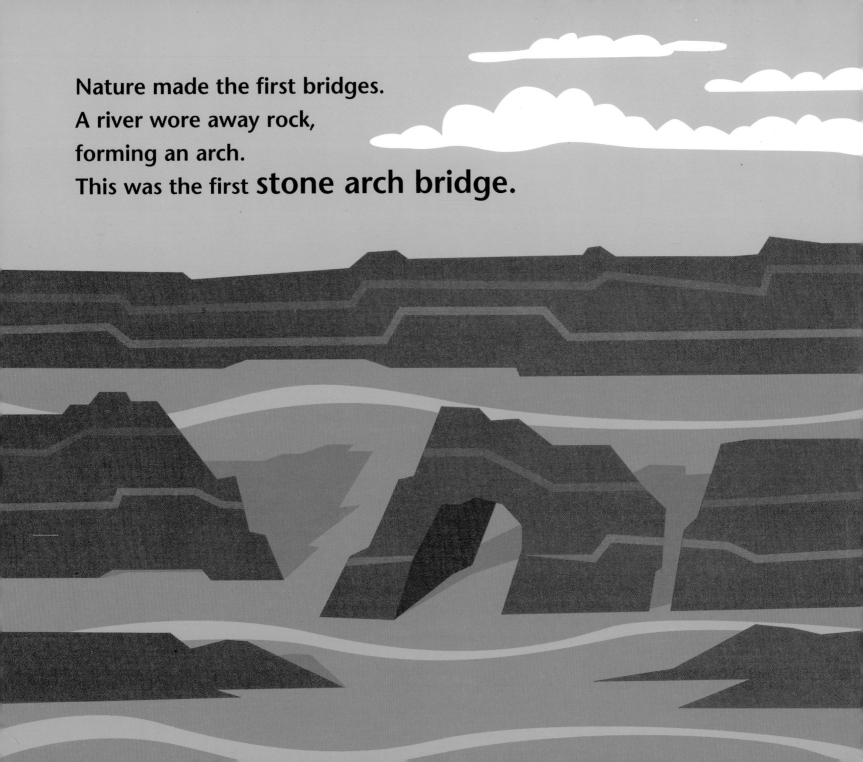

Nature made the first bridges.
A river wore away rock,
forming an arch.
This was the first **stone arch bridge.**

A tree fell across a stream.
Someone chasing an animal
scrambled across it.
This was the first
wood bridge.

Some bridges floated on animal skins
blown up with air, like balloons.
A long time ago, kings sent their armies
into battle across this kind of bridge.
We still use **pontoon bridges,**
only now the pontoons are
usually made of hollowed–out concrete.

Bridges need to be strong.
Some wood bridges were covered
to keep the rain and snow
from rotting the wood.

You can still find old **covered bridges**
on quiet country roads.
When you pass through,
hold your breath
and make a wish.

Trains travel over special bridges called **trestles.**
The braces crisscross underneath the tracks.
They fill the gorge with fantastic patterns.

Suspension bridges are just the opposite. Steel cables crisscross from towers above the bridge. These bridges look like they're hanging right from the sky!

In Colorado you can cross a bridge more than 1,000 feet above the Arkansas River.

Beam bridges are long and flat. They rest on sturdy concrete pilings and reach across lakes and bays. The longest bridges in the world are beam bridges.

One stretches more than 24 miles across
Lake Ponchatrain in New Orleans.
You can't see from one side to the other.

New kinds of bridges are being designed all the time.

Bridges are busy.
They carry cars full of people.
They carry trucks,
busses, and trains, too,
full of people
and all kinds of things
that people need.

Some cities have lots of bridges
to get the cars and trucks,
the busses and trains,
in and out.

If you drive through Paris, you'll have more than thirty bridges to choose from.

Some bridges open up because ships and boats
on the river below are too tall to go under.
Then the cars, trucks,
busses, and trains
just have to wait
while the ships and boats pass through.

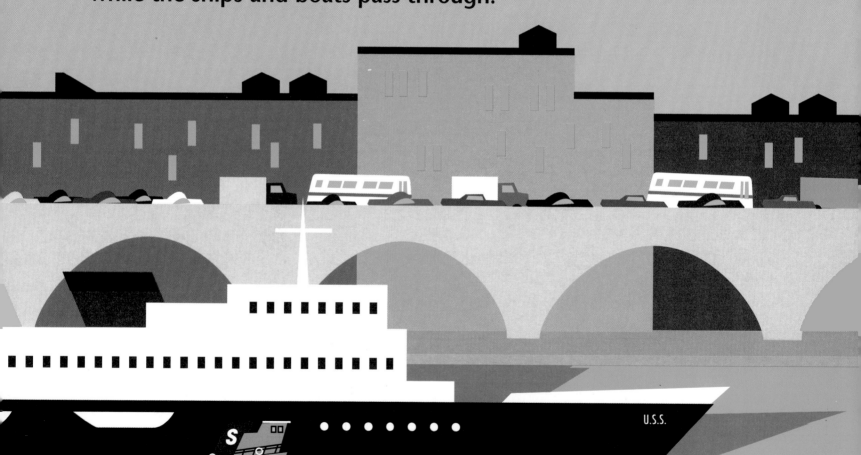

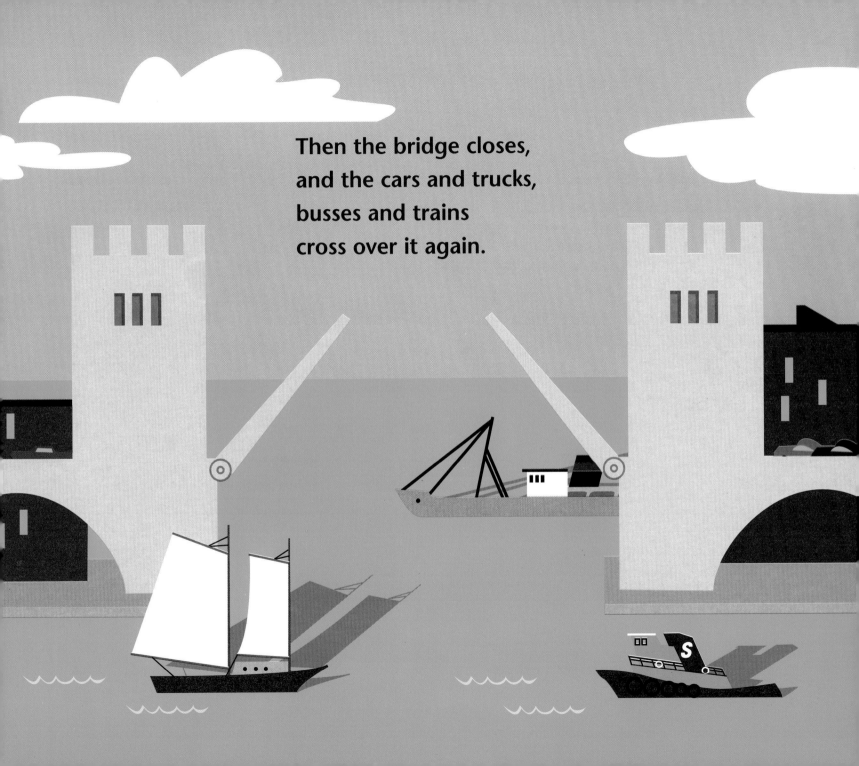

Then the bridge closes,
and the cars and trucks,
busses and trains
cross over it again.

But bridges aren't just for crossing.
Bridges are for sitting,
and fishing,
and wishing.